Lee Aucoin, *Creative Director*
Jamey Acosta, *Senior Editor*
Heidi Fiedler, *Editor*
Produced and designed by
Denise Ryan & Associates
Illustration © Nelle Davis
Rachelle Cracchiolo, *Publisher*

Teacher Created Materials

5301 Oceanus Drive
Huntington Beach, CA 92649-1030
http://www.tcmpub.com
Paperback: ISBN: 978-1-4333-5563-9
Library Binding: ISBN: 978-1-4807-1708-4
© 2014 Teacher Created Materials

Lizzie's Dream

Written by Celia Doyle

Illustrated by Nelle Davis

Lizzie loved looking at the snow-covered mountains she could see from her classroom.

If I could fly over them, I could find out what's on the other side, she thought.

So one day, Lizzie told her friends she was going to be a pilot. Sam told her she would have to be good at math.

"Yes. I will have to work at that," said Lizzie. "I'm not too bad, but I could be better!"

Jen told her she would have to learn all about the planet Earth.

"Hmm. I think I'll need a new atlas," said Lizzie. "Do you think a really big one would help me find out where all the mountains are?"

20 + 5 = 25   12 + 4 = 16

6 During math, Lizzie did all sorts of weird problems. She tried to chart the flight path over the mountains.

"You're supposed to be doing addition," whispered Sam.

"I already finished," said Lizzie. "Now, I'm making a graph. I'm trying to get better at math."

In science class, Mr. Wood showed the students how to make paper airplanes. But Lizzie's plane didn't fly very well.

"I think I need to learn how to fly!" she exclaimed, as her plane crashed onto Jen's head.

When it was silent reading time, Lizzie read a book about the science of flight. Then, she read about spaceships. The next day, she read about the oceans.

Joel whispered to Lizzie, "We're supposed to be reading fiction this week."

"Oh! I forgot! Maybe I should read *The Little Prince*. My friend Cal told me about it. It's a story about a pilot who crashed his plane in northern Africa. It might be a bit sad though."

13

"What book are you reading, Lizzie?" asked Ms. Hale.

"Oh, Ms. Hale," said Lizzie. "I got mixed up. I'm sorry. Joel said I should read *The Way Back Home*. It's about a boy who crashes his airplane on the moon. I think I've read it before, but I love Oliver Jeffers's drawings."

"Once I've read that, I'm going to read *My Life As an Afterthought Astronaut*. Sam said that it's about a boy who stows away on the space shuttle. When he's there, he has to follow the rules. That one's fiction for sure."

The next day, Ms. Hale gave Lizzie three books. "Lizzie, I think you will enjoy reading these," she said. "This book is about Amelia Earhart. Here's one about Bessie Colman, and this one is about Sally Ride. They were all famous pilots."

19

When it was time for silent reading again, Lizzie kept telling Jen about Amelia Earhart.

"She was a pilot and she flew across the Atlantic and she disappeared and…"

"Shhh, Lizzie. We're not supposed to be talking about the books yet."

"Don't call me Lizzie. It's not an astronaut's name. From now on, I'm Liz."

When it was time for math, Liz kept telling Sam all about Bessie Colman. "She was really good at math. She was a stunt flyer and she could…"

"Shhh, Liz. Do your math. We're not supposed to be talking," said Sam.

Later that day, Mr. Wood, showed everyone how to make a rocket. They used paper and fizzing tablets.

When it was finished, Liz asked him, "Do rockets work the same way? They don't use tablets, do they?"

"What do you think, Liz?" asked Mr. Wood.

"I think I need to find out more about rockets," answered Liz. "When I'm an astronaut like Sally Ride, I'm going to fly in a real spaceship. Then, I'll be able to see over the mountains and the oceans, and all around the Earth!"

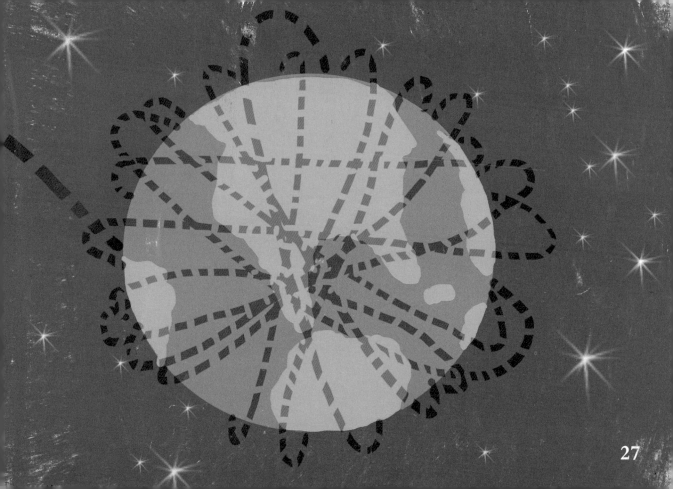

27

"I promise. One day, I'm going to do it! I'm going
to fly over the mountains. Maybe, you can even come
with me!"